Firecrackers

Zaro Weil

illustrated by Jo Riddell

*A smileable, sighable, laugh-out-loudable, gaspable,
dreamable, rappable, singable mix of wild and woolly words
perfect for quiet reading alone, loud reading together,
or wild and woolly performing*

ZaZaKids Books

in association with

Published by ZazaKids Books
in association with
Troika Books

First published in paperback 2020

1 3 5 7 9 10 8 6 4 2

ISBN 978-1-909991-33-0

Designed by Louise Millar

Printed in Poland by Totem www.totem.com.pl

ZazaKids Books
www.zazakidsbooks.com

Troika Books Ltd.
Well House, Green Lane, Ardleigh CO7 7PD, UK
www.troikabooks.com

'A 'Firecracker' by name and by content, this is a real treasure of a book which will soon be a must on all classroom shelves.' *North Somerset Children's Book Group*

'A great collection for sparking the imagination, generating questions, and enjoying the sound and intricacies of language and word play.' *Armadillo Magazine*

'Fun, fantastical and full of variety: a wonderful collection of poems to inspire and delight. Whoopee!!! This bouncy, brilliant book is full of fun.' *BookTrust*

'There is no theme in this enjoyable collection of poems and prose except fun. and there's a lot of whimsical quirkiness.' *The School Librarian*

'Multi-talented Zaro Weil's poems and writing in this book are magical, imaginative and they look at the changing seasons with wonder and awe.' *Wes Magee for Carousel Magazine*

'*Firecrackers* absolutely fizzes and zizzes with over ninety different delights. I strongly believe that poetry should be part of every child's daily experience: teachers there is something for all moods and tastes herein and once you start reading this book with a group of children they'll keep on demanding 'just one more'. Equally it's perfect for the family bookshelf, to set imaginations soaring during the day or to send a child off into dreamworlds of 'sun-dotted butterflies', 'fruit trees in pastel puffs' and shivering crickets.' *Jill Bennett Red Reading Hub*

'*Firecrackers* is a magical and generous new collection of poems, stories and plays. It's beautifully presented and designed with Jo Riddell's wonderful illustrations enhancing the rich array of texts that Zaro Weil has composed'. *Readingzone*

'Beautifully illustrated by Jo Riddell, this collection of poems and stories is a perfect gift book. It's ideal for dipping into, for quiet reading and for reading aloud; indeed, unusually amongst the stories, haiku and poems, there are a couple of rhyming plays too, great fun for the family or a group of friends. Single collections of poems are relatively rare these days, and it's lovely to find one that gives the poet the space and time to explore ideas and return to themes. Poetry speaks to children directly, and this should become a real favourite...' *Love Reading 4 Kids*

'It's difficult to pinpoint who will most enjoy this book – the child or the parent. Because while it will undoubtedly delight the younger reader, it is also chock-full of poems and stories that will appeal to the child in many of us. There are poems short and long and very long. there are stories – some new and some old. And they are all beautifully illustrated by Jo Riddell, whose drawings prove that there is more than one talented artist in her household. I predict that for many, *Firecrackers* will be a book to treasure.' *Poetry Zone*

'*Firecrackers* is a treasure trove of treats! The stunning illustrations feel both fresh and classic, framing a wonderful variety of poetry, word play and stories. This delightful gift hardback is a perfect present, ideal for sharing or cherishing alone.' *Tamara Mcfarlane*

'*Firecrackers* is packed full with explosive words and colourful ideas. The poems range from the pleasingly quirky to the more thoughtful and reflective. There's plenty here that will spark the imagination of a child.' *Rachel Rooney*

For Joseph, Fiona and Arlo

Zaro Weil lives in an old farm on a little hill in southern France. She has been, and continues to be, many things: dancer, theatre director, actress, poet, playwright, educator, antique American quilt collector and historian, author, vegan chef, publisher and a few more.

Her early career was in creative arts education in America. She taught movement, dance, theatre and creative writing to both children and educators in schools, arts centres and at university, while at the same time directing, writing for and performing in the children's theatre dance company Metro Theater Circus which toured throughout America.

Zaro has written a number of highly praised books of children's poetry, plays and stories: *Mud, Moon and Me*, illustrated by Jo Burroughs (now Jo Riddell), published by Orchard Books in the UK and by Houghton Mifflin in the USA; *Firecrackers*, illustrated by Jo Riddell, published by Troika Books; *Spot Guevara, Hero Dog*, illustrated by Katy Riddell, published by Troika Books; and *Cherry Moon*, illustrated by Junli Song, published by Troika Books. *Cherry Moon* was named by *The Independent* as one of the top 30 Children's Books – and the only poetry book included – for 2019.

Her poetry for children has appeared in numerous anthologies.

Jo Riddell has a studio in an old coach house at the bottom of her garden which she shares with her husband Chris. Jo also works at her studio which she shares with Heike Roesel at New England House, Brighton.

After a B.A. degree at Brighton University she worked in children's books, publishing twelve books over ten years.

Since returning to printmaking and painting she has found a welcome freedom to express herself, inspiration coming from family, found objects, and the landscapes of Sussex and Norfolk

Acknowledgements

Many of the poems, plays, raps and haiku in this book have been lovingly read, sung, danced and acted by friends and colleagues over the years. I am grateful always for their continued warmest of friendships and support. In particular I thank Jane O Wayne, Carol Evans North, Nick Kryah, Branislav Tomich and June Ekman.

Judith Elliott has been an extraordinary, caring and brilliant editor.

My friends at Troika have been a joy to work with.

I heartily thank the amazing Jo Hardacre who provides dynamic publicity support for all of my books.

Jo Riddell embraced *Firecrackers* with remarkable sensitivity and made it her own. I could not have wished for a more perfect illustrator.

Gareth Jenkins has patiently lived with me and this book for many years, steadfast in his encouragement while kindly suggesting spot-on critiques.

For these friends, colleagues and family, I count my lucky stars.

Contents

Long ages ago

Long ages ago
in ancient earth time
creatures talked like us
but in wacky weird rhyme

They'd jibber and jabber
of what they were wearing
what this one was doing
how that one was faring

They'd gossip like crazy
things of no matter
then utter dumb jokes
to keep up their chatter

They never did quit
all night and all day
till the sound of their voices
drove the world to dismay

The sun roared 'PLEASE STOP'
the moon covered its ears
hid behind clouds
and burst into tears

The stars were aghast
the wind just astounded
and planets that circled
plunged down and were grounded

This couldn't continue
something had to get going
to stop all these beasts
from their noisy outflowing

'Aha' cried the sun
'I know what to do'
so she summoned them all
the old and the new

Everyone came
from the ants to the bats
the elephants, hedgehogs
fish, birds, and rats

Once they were gathered
from monkeys to pups
the sun sent down her rays
 commanding 'shut up'

The silence was huge
until the sun muttered
'I can stand this no more
rhymes may not be uttered

'Listen you creatures
you have too much to say
and it's time you stopped talking
like humans this way

'To be really important
to be really you
you must not sound like
you know very well who'

'But Sun' they all cried
'you're far too imperious
if we didn't talk rhyme
we'd blip flip delirious'

'Not at all' said the sun
in a warming up tone
'it's important to speak
in a voice that's your own

'Now cats try to purr
pigeons coo-coo
dogs learn how to bark
and cows just say moo

'Lions must roar
donkeys hee-haw
elephants trumpet
and crows please say caw'

It continued this way
there was really no choice
with each animal trying
to find its own voice

At the end of that day
it was quite understood
that the animals sounded
much more like they should

And so it went on
years passed by through time
till no beast remembered
they used to speak rhyme

Now if you don't believe
that this story is fact
just go ask the sun
wherever she's at

She'll tell you the truth
for it's part of earth's way
that funny weird rhyme
won't quite go away

And if even that
doesn't really convince you
take a moment to listen
to an old dog or two

Hear when they speak
and go bark bark bark bark
if you pay close attention it's

Hark mark
the lark in
the park

Wake up

Wake up
morning
has
galloped
bareback
all night to
get here

Think of it

The first shudder of damp
somehow signalled
all was ready
then in the deep inside of earth
in the muted underneath of winter
spring began

Not with a sudden trumpet of green
or a sky of confetti blossoms
but with a seed
small pale and barely breathing

It lay quietly
waiting for lavender clouds
that carry the first warm rains
till for some reason
as ancient and everyday
as the sun itself

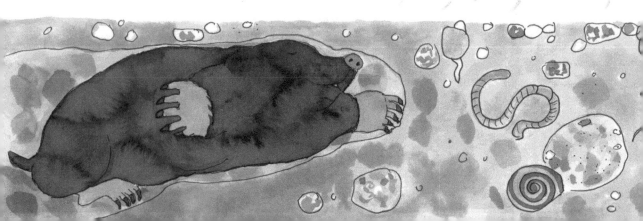

The seed cracked
split and softly burst into
a faint tendril
a root a sprout
a thin wisp of a growing thing

And with no thought of stopping
it pushed through the
dark soil with the force of
a billion winter winds
until it

Pierced the crust of outside and
split the frozen armour of earth
which has held spring safe
since time began

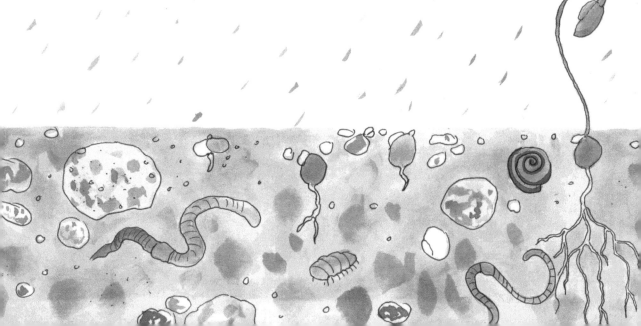

The Sun Queen

morning

When she was very young, she believed
the sun rose the instant she opened her eyes
in the morning. Often, she tried to fool
the sun, by opening her eyes one at a time.
But the sun was always there. Loyal to her.
And she realised she was Queen of the Sun.

She Rise Sun

Sun Yes your majesty

She Shine Sun

Sun Yes, your majesty

She Warm me

Sun A pleasure

She And Sun

Sun Yes

She Make this a zoo day

Sun I'll certainly try, my Queen

She Good

How to get an idea

Dig into mud

   or

Open up a new box of crayons

   or

Run your finger through a bag of marbles

   or

Skip a stone across water

   or

Ask a cat to lend you one

   or

Stand quietly under a dictionary

   or

Stick out your tongue and say, 'O!'

   or

Put an empty picture frame on the wall
   and wait

At the iron bridge

Not quite spring
but at the iron bridge
there is water

It happened last night
in a flash
swelling without a trace to
thunder this morning
down from the mountains
fresh
from underground streams
cold
from moonlight rains
expectant
frothing

First a mindless whirl
next an endless rush
heading always
to the river
now surging
pouring over pyramids of rock
shaved smooth
by other water
other times

Only slowing
to seep into a few fat pools
mini lakes full of
tiny living things
new things
strange things
skimming oh so fast
over green surfaces
racing through tangles of vines
floating twigs
last summer's snaky
brown grasses

And all the while
early mist
gleams through the
haze of morning bright sun
adding to the shiny wetness
of everything

Yet these events
this timeless cycle
of earth and sky
means nothing to
two dogs
who fly
into the water
bright squeals and paddling paws
ears wiggling
tongues flapping
yelping
barking unrestrained delight

Finally unleashed from winter
and desperate to catch that first
splash of spring
in their own
timeless cycle

After the storm

After the storm
the sun slinks in
all purrs and soft paws
but the sky
stays red and puffy
remembering rain

Snail

Snail crept by my toe
antennae out
torso stretched
seeking a squelchy spot

unlike me

On the lookout

Dogs are always
on the lookout
sniffing
pawing the ground
carpet
grass
seeking morsels
bugs
information
sometimes serious
or a game to be played

But always in earnest
convinced there is nothing
more important in the world
than this search
knowing something is hidden
waiting just for them

Put off by nothing
even a flash – dashing hare
orange fox
or jumpy grasshopper
won't budge them
from their hot pursuit

Nor does it matter that they
don't find whatever it is
they are quite capable of turning on a dime
having a scratch
a bark that means business
to head off tails full mast
ears cocked
to new territory
to be tasted examined
rolled in

While we humans
drift through our days
mostly in a dog's slow motion
concerned with our everyday things
'have to do' things
and maybe just a bit
removed from being really

on the scent

Comet

The night crackles with silence
as you fly
headlong among the stars
against dark granite
you are a spray of hot gold
fiery plume of an ancient creature
frivolous stroke of a molten pen
breathless orange curve
you cut through boundless sky
a determined race to the future
a dazzle of a second
a moment of the past

A field of daffodils

A field of daffodils
hundreds
thousands
and no basket
large enough
for April

Two sun-dotted butterflies

Outside my bedroom window
two sun-dotted butterflies
rush in rolling cyclones
around the still yawning garden as
four yellow wings
push the pale morning air
this way and that
fluttering endless circles
inside out of each other
over and over in
an electrifying chase
only slowing to land
with no trace
no sound
on a just-born tendril of something blue
where without seeming to move at all
they suck something wonderful

and start again

Tiny moon

Tiny moon
even a
penny
could eclipse you
this morning

The paper bag

Fill up a paper bag with
spring sounds and
open it in December

Fill up a paper bag with
snow flurries and
use them to decorate your bedroom

Fill up a paper bag with
ribbons and
fly them when you want a word with the wind

Fill up a paper bag with
winter quiet
and open it when it's time to be alone
Fill up a paper bag with
your favourite words and
shake it till a good story comes out

Fill up a paper bag with
secrets and
share them with a friend every so often

Fill up a paper bag with
velvet
just to have it

It's Monday

It's Monday   my sore hurts

It's Tuesday   my hair is growing

It's Wednesday my hands are clean

It's Thursday   my muscle is big

It's Friday   my tongue touches my nose

It's Saturday   my legs turn cartwheels

It's Sunday   my arm grew a freckle

It's Monday   I'm still me

                   only more

The field near my house

Now ragged
threadbare and browning,
the field near my house was once
a slaphappy place —
where every flower, weed, blade of grass
was impossibly bright, far too tall
helplessly tangled.

Where birds lured by the lucky infinity
of seeds and nectar grew summer fat,
where a million speckled and lined bugs
careened purposefully this way and that,
living their short little lives
drenched in the special scents
the painted bliss of this field.

But then,
when no one was looking,
everything browned
sank and collapsed.

Wildlife headed south,
crept into hollows
till only the wind was left
pausing for nothing
and even the sun
grew chilled by degrees.

Walking slowly,
I note half-buried
some wisp of forgotten green —
a petal of brittle rose
pasted to a broomstick
of last season's vine.

And in one gasp drawn sharp,
I recall that time —
the rainbow revels in this same field
and wait
like the barely breathing roots,

one thought in mind.

So much wind

So much wind
all outside ruffles
as autumn sways
and nothing
flies straight

Let's run away
a rappy shaggy sheepdog play

SPOT   hey there sis
let's run away
slip outside
whaddaya' say
come on come on
there's no more day
moon's coming out
sun's going away
it'll be super great
we won't hesitate
hate running straight
we can approximate
slip through the gate
then navigate
it's our doggie fate
they'll make a fuss
but won't find us
we'll take off
scadooddle
fly with the wind
won't be fenced in
let's race over rocks

42

who needs socks
never look at clocks
doncha' really wanna be
pawloose and free
come on sis
just you and me

CLEMENTINE   OK, Spot
let's go!
whooooaaa.
what a great romp
through the woods
feeling mighty good
'cos it's our 'hood
could do anything
we would we would
my brother and me
movin' so fast
having a blast
eight paws racin'
tongue and ears facin'
the starry night air
not one little care
such an awesome pair
pant pant pant
that's our wild dog chant
sniff sniff sniff

43

that's our sheepdog riff

bow wow wow

'cos we know how

passing bats and bees

chasing off fleas

having lots of pees

hey brother

keep up with me please

it's cooler than cool

like breakin' out of school

no humans to obey

tired of doing what they say

don't wanna sit

hate the word stay

SPOT   yeh

we're two crazy dogs

let's find us some hogs

chase those ugly wild boars

who go on all fours

they're mean and hairy

supersonic scary

with huge great snouts

always wearin' pouts

sprouting razor sharp tusks

can smell 'em by their musk
their horns would tear you apart
without thinking twice
from your tail to your heart
you'd be spliced
sliced
totally diced

CLEMENTINE   stop Spot
don't bark such rot
that's not
gonna happen to you and me
get it brother
this is key
wait a minute
something's around
I can tell from the sound

SPOT   I can tell from the smell
take a peek what's moving
in the forest Clem
wow
I can count ten
no ten times ten
better count 'em again
look

all those big hairy beasts

are having a feast

munchin' everything in sight

in the middle of night

let's go pull their shaggy tails

tug on a horn

make 'em wish

they'd never been born

CLEMENTINE   no

listen up Spot

we gotta be smart

gotta be shifty

gotta make those boars retreat

it'll be super nifty

let's pretend we're a pack

like we're gonna attack

like we're chasin' them back

we'll bark and bark and bark

they don't see well in the dark

and with their squinty little eyes

it'll be a surprise

and with our most ferocious howls

we'll sound like

beasts on the prowl

with vicious snarling jowls
what a tricky sly way
to make those monsters
run away

SPOT ha ha ha
love it Clem
what a super good plan
shhhhhh
just listen to 'em snort
listen to those stamps
what horrible obnoxious
oinking mean rants
now let's bark
like we're a hundred
hounds on the loose
ready to attack
and cook their goose
but wait have a care
we better stay hidden
behind those
trees over there

SPOT & CLEMENTINE	OK let's get 'em woof woof woof grr grr grr ahoo ahoo ahoo bow wow wow snarl grunt grumble boars you're gonna be rumbled roar bellow thunder boars your days are numbered bray yip yap yelp belt snap bam pow shazam double triple scram stay offa' our patch get outta' our woods 'cos we're a hundred mighty hounds with horrible mean sounds gonna rip you apart and that's just a start
CLEMENTINE (*whispering*)	hey Spot whaddya' think can we stop this now

my throat's getting sore
do we really need
to keep barking more

SPOT   Clem what a great trick
look over there quick
we scared 'em off good
see how fast they're running
outta the wood
wow
and the likelihood
is they wouldn't dare
they're far too scared
to come back and fight us
mighty dogs in plain air

CLEMENTINE   what a brilliant lark
when they heard us bark
when they heard our yips
those big boar losers
cleared off in a snip
they turn into wimps
it would clearly seem
when they're up against
our great brother and sister team

SPOT	yeh sis
	but sort of feeling hungry
	sort of feeling tired
	think it's just about time
	to head on home
	to dinner and a bone
CLEMENTINE	hey
	mom'll give us lots of cookies
	call us cute little schnookies
SPOT	and in our cosy soft beds
	we'll rest our brave doggie heads
	and dream of our great fight
	so woof woof woof to all
SPOT &	and to all an
CLEMENTINE	heroic
	tail waggy
	ears flappy
	totally happy
	good night

51

This bed is so fat

This bed is so fat
this pillow so soft
hundreds of dreams
can climb right in

Seal

Seal sits on the rock
barely a shuffle all day
sunny water laps his fur
salt sprays his whiskers
watching uninvited
wind slaps my face

Hushed and buried

Buried and hushed
till one morning
fields turn over
rainbows on earth

the suddenness of spring

Swallows

Twilight
tiny crescents
circle
dive
a hundred sky games

naturally
moon wins

If I lived in Giggleswick Town

If I lived in Giggleswick town
I'd wake up each morning
as the sun goes down

Stars would pop out at noon each day
while the moon laughed its head off
at whatever I'd say

Songs would sprout from every roof
and I'd sing with them all
and be a big goof

Next I'd go flying on two coloured wings
swish everywhere
and become everything

I'd swoop past the hills and over the sea
make friends with the wind
and joke with the trees

We'd have our own club the forest and I
and we'd invite all the creatures
who'd ever passed by

We'd break into smiles, dream up some lines
then wiggle our roots
with each silly rhyme

Soon everyone there would be talking nonstop
telling funny tall tales
sipping pink soda pop

We'd shout and we'd snort a million wild words
then stomp up and down
like elephant herds

We'd giggle so hard the creatures and me
letters would give up
fly off and be free

Up they'd all zoom like rockets through space
and it's then that I'd know

I love this place

Ferocious rumpus siggles

Wildiggly roars

This fig

This fig has

so much sun

the whole summer

bursts in my mouth

at the first bite

Where it's at

a little play

For a very long time, in fact ever since time had a name and lived on earth, all creatures argued about which one of them was the most important; the centre of . . . well . . . everything. They named this centre where it's at. Discussions about where it's at went on year after terrible year. Arguments grew. Bitter fights emerged.

BEE   Buzzy big buzz! Where it's at is me and whatever flower I land upon. You see brilliant yours truly gets to decide. That's how important I am.

SPIDER   Wrong, bee. Where it's at is not on any of your smelly flowers. Where it's at is me when I spin my beautiful web. Why don't you pass this way, know-it-all bee? Come on.

CRICKET   Get a life! Where it's at is me making out-of-tune grating noises every minute of the day and night. Ah. It's getting hot. Time to begin. I love rubbing my fabulous little legs together. I am so where it's at. Graaaaaatttteeeee graaaaatttteee....

NIGHTINGALE Crazy cricket! You don't know the first thing. Where it's at is me when I sing under the moon. No creature can tweet a more beautiful song than me. Get ready world…Do re mi fa sol la ti doooooo…

WILD BOAR Rubbish and giant smelly tiddlywinks, nightingale! Where it's at is not a boring little brown bird like you. No, it is me when I go snorting and digging in the earth to get those delicious, ugly earthworms.

EARTHWORM Ugly? What do you know, big brute boar? You giant lug. I am going to wrap myself around your long nose next time and squeeze harder than hard. You don't scare me. I may be small but I am the most where it's at creature in the universe.

KING OF   ROAR . . .

BEASTS   Quiet! I have heard enough. Where it's at is me, since I am king of everything. Everyone knows that. And if you don't believe me I'll roar my head off again and gobble you all up for dinner.

SNAKE   Shhhhhhhhhhhhh. Hissssssssss. Look, nitwitssssss, where it's at is my slithery self when I slide oh so fast in between the tall grasses. Now quiet. All of you. I smell something. Here, mousssssssyyyyyy.

The terrible fighting and bickering went on and on. One day the beasts got so fed up and angry that they decided to ask a human to help them decide. They had to know which one of them was the most important where it's at animal. After anxiously searching the globe, they found a human who made pictures which looked like their world. He was called artist. The animals thought the artist's pictures looked pretty good and figured this human must know a thing or two.

ANIMALS   Artist, you see the world very well. Tell us once and for all which one of us is the most important where-it's-at creature on earth.

ARTIST   Hmm. A hard question, but I think I can figure it out.

The artist picked up a blank piece of paper. He took a brush, dipped it in ink and made a blue circle with a red dot in the centre. He took another piece of paper and did the same thing but with different colours. He painted an orange circle with a purple dot. And then a yellow circle with a green dot. And then another. He painted more and more circles and dots until the ground was covered with paintings of circles and dots in a hundred colours.

SPIDER   Come on, artist. That's enough of your pictures. The circles and dots all look alike. Stop painting and give us the answer. Which one of us is where it's at? I haven't got all day.

ARTIST   Don't you get it? Where it's at is every one of you. You are ALL right.

SPIDER: Artist, are you nuts?

CRICKET   You've got to be kidding.

ARTIST   No. Each picture is as important as the next one. Just as each of you is as important as everyone else.

NIGHTINGALE Are you saying that we are ALL where it's at?

ARTIST   Yes.

WILD BOAR   Artist, that is one crazy idea and you are one ridiculous artist.

SPIDER	I never liked that artist anyway.
LION	Grrrrrrr. I think I might gobble him up.
ARTIST	Don't you get it? You are all as important as your fellow creatures.
EARTHWORM	Now I've heard everything. This is definitely nuts.
CRICKET	What do you expect from a human?
BEE	Look, artist. I think you'd better take off before something very bad happens to you.

With that the artist shrugged his shoulders and walked off. The animals angrily vowed never to ask a human anything ever again. But as they looked up into the noonday sky a new idea popped into their heads. A brilliant idea. A fabulous idea. They would ask someone who really would know. The sun!

Yes, they agreed.
The sun sees everything. Goes everywhere.
Is the centre of the universe, in fact.
The sun will be sure to know who is where it's at on earth.

And chattering and whining and arguing nonstop,
off they each raced to be the very first to find the sun.

CODA

BEE	Oh suuuuunnnnn.
SPIDER	You whoooo? Remember me, sun?
LION	Grrrrr. I saw her first.
SNAKE	No. Itsssssss meeeee.
BOAR	Snort. She likes me best.
NIGHTINGALE	She loves my music. She told me so.
CRICKET	But she promised me I was the only where-it's-at beastie this morning.

And on and on and on and on . . .

A boy and his dog

Boy	Here dog
Dog	WOOF
Boy	Good dog
Dog	WOOF WOOF
Boy	Now sit
Dog	WOOF WOOF WOOF
Boy	Now stand
Dog	WOOF WOOF WOOF WOOF
Boy	Roll over
Dog	WOOF WOOF WOOF WOOF WOOF
Boy	Now speak
Dog	Here boy

When I was the sunrise

When I was

the

sunrise

sunset

used

to

wait

for

me

every

day

When I was the sunset

When I was

the

sunset

sunrise

used

to

wait

for

me

every

night

Seasonal rites

An epic chaos
light against dark
the muddy push-pull
of winter and spring
I consider myself lucky
stealing a dry hour
from these seasonal rites

My two sheepdogs
noses twitching of March
fur ruffing
bound down a path by the lake

Back and forth
finding me
losing me

Unleashed revellers they leap
over piles of hollow reeds
soggy ribbons of vines
all emptied of summer

At breakneck speed
they chase one another
through clumps of brambles
rotted tree stumps
spiky weeds
a ritual frenzy of grabbing
ears muzzles tails

Panting
mouths open
tongues lolling
something else draws them
a new orgy

They sniff wild leeks
inch-high daisies
till possessed of nose-to-tail glee
they jump full tilt
into the lake
paddling rings
in the mirrored water

Lured by a sudden note
of sheep in the air
they clamber out and
delirious with expectation
race over a moonscape of
jagged rocks

Some strangers pass

The dogs
wild-eyed creatures now
drenched in brown slime
drunk with freedom
stop in their tracks
ceaselessly barking

their own rite of spring

Owl's haiku

Waiting
stillness rules
will the moon appear
tonight
will my shadow soar

Skunk's haiku

Don't be shy
come close
I promise to be good
look
tail's down

April fool!

New shoes

New shoes
take me out
this morning
the day begins
so fresh and polished

Cotton slow rain

Cotton slow rain
cotton slow day
a tan and striped chipmunk
taps the door
what?

a party?

A bird concert

A bird concert
lengthens the day
while that frog chorus
waits for the moon

so impatient

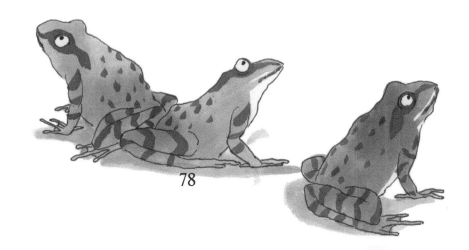

Once there were two bears

an American rap in three parts

Part 1

once there were two bears
too small for any scares
just a fluffy soft pair
of cubs without a care
always hunting for fare
in a hurry
eight paws scurry scurry
loping faster than air
needing more than honey
to fill their cub tummies
both lookin' to tear
open any trash
anxious for a stash
could be a mouldy old pear
covered in hair
leftovers well done
or cooked kind of rare
they'd prowl through trees
arrive at towns and cities
run a hundred laps
to find rotting scraps

they loved their treats
could eat and eat and eat
from dusk till dawn
and when the moon was gone
as the sun got high
those cubs would sigh
start to cry
start to howl
start to growl
feeling hungry and
had to go out again
on the prowl
they'd wait till night
no people in sight
not one shred of light
and in the dark
when no dogs bark
they did things right
with a heave and some hails
they'd empty those pails
and straight through the garbage
they'd slip and sail
where goopy kale
dead pizza prevailed
rooting through the bags

spread out all over
could have been clover
but it wasn't
it was gross
disgusting and smelly
good for bear's belly
now all over the lawns
but while munching old prawns
two kids full of yawns
came out from their house

Part 2

hey is that a fawn
is that a hare
who's that making
such a racket out there
we say who's there
ring two voices
clear as a bell
and opening the door
both kids see the cubs and yell
stop bears
put that back

that's dad's trash sack
clean up mom's yard
get that mess off the grass
do it fast or
mom will get mad
dad will get madder

but kids growl the cubs
this stuff makes us gladder than gladder
we love your garbage
can't get enough
we gotta chomp through it all
we're havin' a ball

see we're growin' stout
growin' tall
oh my gosh we are totally wowed
are you little bears
really talking out loud
hey what are you two called
ask the kids now enthralled
my name is Molly
I'm called Gus
giggle two cubs with a cute furry blush.
well bears
do you think you'd like to play with us
don't rightly know can't rightly say
but all wonder to themselves

do cubs and kids
play together these days

now Molly and Gus are very friendly
run up to the steps
where the kids are standing
hi kids say the cubs landing
just below their feet
we'd love to play won't be rough
do you know hide and seek
or blind man's bluff

and in the blink of an eye
off the four of them run
around the messed-up garden
having loads of fun
they spin and laugh
about a thousand times
till all four are worn out
and the kids call
time out
but then they start to pout
what's the matter ask the cubs
why you looking so sad
'cos when they see this mess
when they see this trash
all over the place
mom's gonna groan
dad'll make a bad face
and we don't know when
we'll get to play with you again

Part 3

Molly and Gus grow quiet
count to ten and then
don't worry they shout

we have a plan
we'll eat what we want
then clean up every can
so off they both race
off they both travel
collecting garbage off the grass
off the gravel
they put it all into sacks
fill up each bin
and soon that garden
is as neat as a pin
hooray they both shout
let's play together again
awesome cry the kids
but here's what we'll do
we'll always leave out
some yummy dinner for you
mom's a good cook
doesn't need a book
do you bears like

strawberry shortcake
gingerbread
hot dogs with mustard and sauerkraut
buttermilk biscuits

macaroni and cheese
blueberry pancakes
corn-on-the-cob
chocolate birthday cake
oatmeal cookies
apple pie

are you kidding
cry the cubs with two greedy bear sighs
but hey is this all a tease
a silly human wheeze
no shout the kids
you gotta believe us please
now how 'bout spaghetti
peanut butter and jelly
hot dog and yippee
that'll fill our bear bellies

so that's how it was
that's how it went down
every time Molly and Gus came to town
they'd gobble down dishes
fit for a king
then with the kids
they'd party play and sing
now at that lucky house
forever and after
you could hear lots and lots
and lots of laughter
the bears and kids
are still best best friends
and it's all because of
that smelly
disgusting
slimy
gooey
gross
wonderful
american garbage
in the end

This wet spring moon

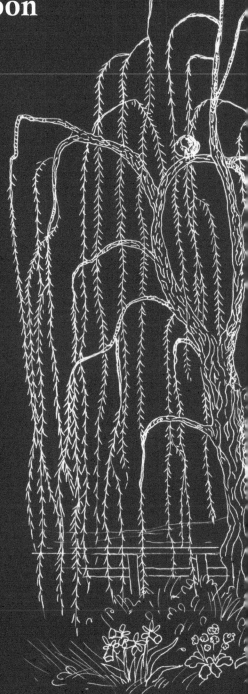

This wet spring moon
sits perched
trapped
under an enormous
dark cloud

Oh so pale
barely balanced
it waits
as the sodden puff
furiously unrolls into
a potato-faced stranger
untamed dragons
twenty fast flying fish

While back on earth
birds hastily retreat
into moist feathered balls
earthworms stretch
dank tunnels
through oozy thick clods
and flat-footed snails
appear everywhere
a thousand sticky trails

Till with not
one sound
nor backwards glance
the cloud vanishes

for the storm has passed

Silver streamers
unfurl over the garden
painted blossoms
burst from quivering buds
countless scents rise
from buried places
as this wet spring moon

grows ripe

Nightingale's haiku

Hidden
I woo the night
note by note till
galaxies twirl
stars applaud

Hare's haiku

Hop
hop
stop
I hear it all
wind
sun
fat roll of clouds

whoops
time to go

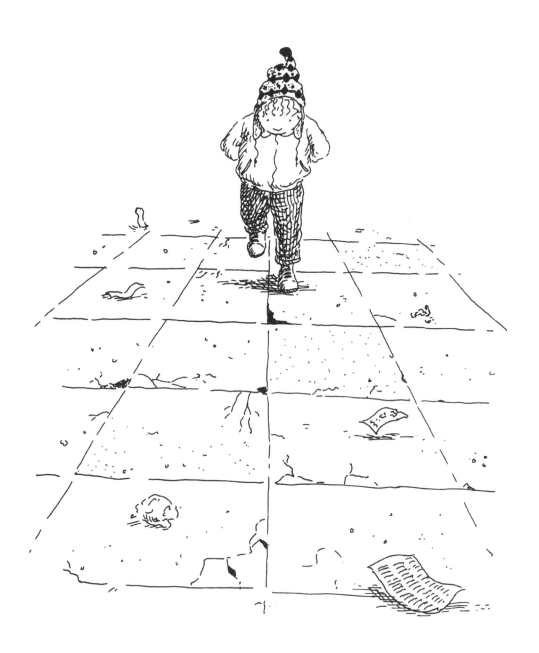

The sidewalk

Count the spots
and the lines
the crooked designs
the lacing of here to there
the colours of threads
in directions of webs
paper scraps
bumps and cracks
that form into rows
of curves that go
into puzzles
I solve
very slowly

Two cats

Two pussycats
playing
pawed in my
snow garden
arching
circling
rolling like it was
summer and
goldenrod had
flown in their noses

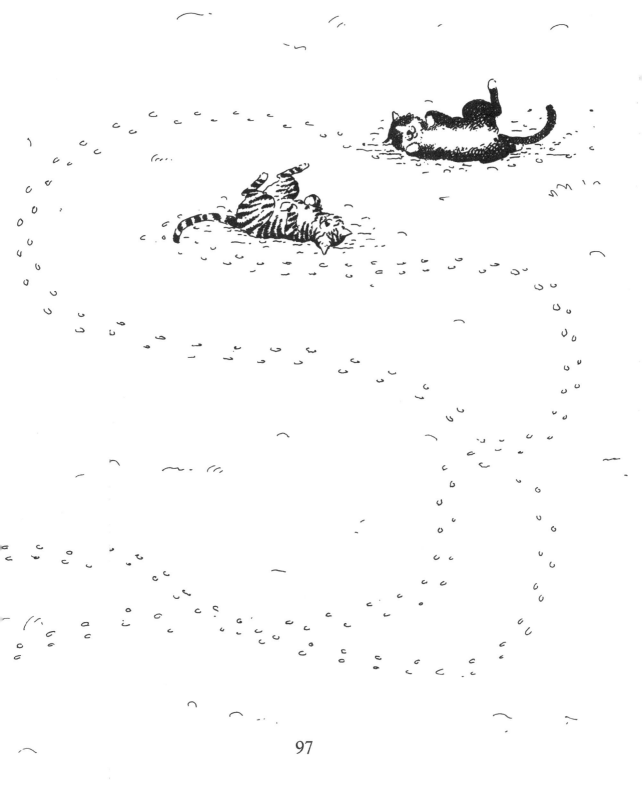

The car ride

Boy   Why are you racing, trees?

Trees   Because you are-r-r-r-r-r-r-r.

Boy   But look. I'm sitting still!

Trees   That's what you think-k-k-k-k.

Boy   Well, last one to the traffic light is a monkey's uncle!

Trees   You're on-n-n-n-n-n.

Truffle dogs

Each morning I wait
for that tangle of
silky damp paws
smelling of yesterday's earth and sunset
encrusted with the remains
of last summer
to leap onto my bed
and paw
the pillow mountains
till two cold noses
root out
my sleepy ear
and quick flicking tongues
cover me with a hundred
let's go outside licks

The baby owl

Arriving home,
the sun still hot and
runny as molasses –
my eyes stick to something lying fast
on the rough pebbles.
'It can't be. It can't be.'
My voice falls in a clump to the ground
upon spotting a baby owl
half on its back –
half in yesterday's dark side.
An uneven fistful of grey and white.
Once so symmetrical,
so laced with wind –
now a distant thing altogether.
A lump with tiny cold claws and beak.
Nothing moving.
Just a small swarm of shadows
– my own –
circling the dead bird.
Runny as molasses,
but not as sweet.

Midnight

One nightingale
in quiet woods
moon sings so loud
dawn hesitates

August heat

August heat
covers everything
silences minutes
muffles the day

summer snow

Donkey's haiku

Hee haw

hee haw

best words to bray

poetry sublime

what?

sure

one more time

Cat's not quite haiku

Meowowowowowow
you may keep staring
I might stretch soon
flick my tail
even lick my paws

wowowowowowme

Finally mud

Finally mud
the first warm rains
fruit trees in pastel puffs
sprinkle the countryside
candy floss season

Blue moon

Blue moon
full moon
no dogs bark
no wolves howl
magic rises

no hiding

Lizard's haiku

Dudes

it reeks
stinks
festering piles
ain't nothin more cool
garbage

dig it

Walking the dogs

Oozy red mud
sparkling green mint
woody smells
under my shoes

When barking at all things
exciting on the still
steaming path
my dogs hot foot it over
to some spider webs –
little lace blankets
on fallen leaves –
so new
so rain shiny
dazzling really

And I had
almost missed them
this tiny flashback
of last night's
tempest

From my window

The water falls in rectangles
cities sprout umbrellas
clear water paints a blurred picture
tears slide from afternoon branches
dirt breathes a deep sigh of mud

it's raining today

My dream day

Wigglesome puppies are a waking up must
then brushing my teeth with silly-time dust
getting dressed in a story of faraway places
and wearing new shoes with milk chocolate laces

I fly on a kitten to my perfect tree house
and write funny poems with a soft little mouse
the snowman outside never melts down or falls
and the trees draw tall pictures all over the walls

I giggle and bounce down a trampoline road
and meet up with clowns and a wish-making toad
he asks where I want to be in my dreams
and I answer: where nothing is as it seems

Where days are bright lollies you never stop licking
and the night wildflowers you never stop picking
where friends are all happy to come over and play
and we laugh and turn into whatever we say

I am a lion with a big yellow roar
a tiger, an elephant, a crocodile and more
the moon whispers and shines a thousand big riddles
with answers found only in earth's deepest middle

By now it is late and I head back to bed
which is fluffy and chewy and liquorice red
my eyes flutter close, my giggles calm down
off to dream of those puppies and cartwheeling clowns

The three little pigs
a rhyming play

Once upon a time, when pigs spoke rhyme
And monkeys chewed tobacco
And hens took snuff to make them tough
And ducks went quack, quack, quack O

There was an old sow now
I don't mean a cow now
Who wore a pink wig
And had three little pigs

> PIG 1   Fat

> PIG 2   Fatter

> PIG 3   Fattest

One day Mama said

MAMA PIG   I love you all three
                    All three I do

ALL PIGS   And Mama

They squealed

ALL PIGS   We love you too

Well they kissed and hugged
And danced all around
Oinked and made some happy pig sounds
A chortle a churtle
A gurgle and squeal
Turned in circles and kicked their heels

Now it must have come as quite a surprise
When Mama grew silent and with misty eyes called

MAMA PIG   Little piglets, piglets three
　　　　　　　　Come sit close to me

ALL PIGS   But Mama, why are you talking so seriously

MAMA PIG   Because it's time it's time You're old enough
　　　　　　　　You're all looking piggy, plump and stuffed
　　　　　　　　It's time it's time for you to leave home
　　　　　　　　Piglets three, you're on your own

ALL PIGS   Oh Mama

They exclaimed in most urgent of tones

ALL PIGS   We love it here Mama
　　　　　　　　This is our home

They cajoled coaxed begged and whined
They pleaded and pouted

MAMA PIG   I won't change my mind
              You see all creatures must leave home some time

Well sadly they left with a tear and a sigh
Waved goodbye to their old pigsty
To that safe and warm place they waved goodbye
They didn't notice Mama with the tear in her eye
But just as they were treading out the front gate
Mama turned around and hollered

MAMA PIG   Wait

All four locked in a warm embrace
And Mama with concern all over her face said

MAMA PIG   Remember this and hear me well
              You must all find a home to safely dwell
              We pigs have an enemy who's mean and tough
              You can recognise him by his huff and his puff
              He'll pretend to be friendly and wear a wide grin
              But he's a WOLF and he'll eat you
              by my chinny chin chin

The pigs smiled bravely

ALL PIGS   Ha ha ha Mama we'll be OK

But down inside each was scared to go
And they didn't want the others to know

PIG 1   Heck Mama

PIG 2   Aw Mama

PIG 1   Don't worry about me

PIG 2   If I meet the wolf then one two three

PIG 1   I'll let him know who's the boss

PIG 2   I'll pull on his nose

PIG 1   He'd better watch out

PIG 2   'Cos pigs are tough as well as stout

MAMA PIG   Enough enough

PIG 3   Don't fear for us, Mama we won't be alone
We'll protect ourselves
We'll build a new home

One last hug was passed around
And then the pigs were on their own

ALL   Bye bye

After they'd been walking
They all began talking
One to another

PIG 1 Sister and brother here's a good spot
        A solid plot of land on which to build
        Now my best guess is that our house
        Should face the west

PIG 2 Sister I don't agree
        'Cos south is where I'd like to be

PIG 3 Wait a minute if we build a place
        east is where I'd like to face

They argued and shouted all that day
All three tried to get their way
The third pig tried to stop the row
But the other two pigs just stepped on his toe . . . ow

PIG 1 Leave us alone

PIG 2 We know what we want

119

And off each went with an oink and a grunt
Well there was nothing more to do or say
So the third little pig she went away
Now the youngest little pig off she did trundle
When she came across some straw in a bundle
She stopped and paused and raised a hoof

PIG 1   I'll use this straw for a house with a roof
      And it's very very very clear
      My house should face exactly here

Well she built that house in a minute or two
And when that first little pig was through
She stood and smiled

PIG 1   Say this looks good
          I've got the best place in the neighbourhood

She kicked up her hooves and did a roll
And into the front door she did stroll

PIG 2   Humph

Said the second pig from where he had stood

PIG 2   That's not so good
          I'm going to build mine here out of wood
          Yes indeed indeedy yes
          My house my house is gonna be the best

He built that house in a minute or three
And then the middle pig shouted

PIG 2   Wheeeeee

He kicked up his hooves and did a roll
And into the front door he did stroll

PIG 3   Hmmmmmmmmmmm..

The oldest pig thought out loud

PIG 3   My brother and sister are certainly proud
         Listen piglets hear what I say
         Straw and sticks won't keep the wolf away

PIGS 1 and 2   Ha ha ha sister don't you see
               You're jealous 'cos you don't have a house like me

The third pig thought and thought

PIG 3   Sticks and straws straws and sticks
         I'm gonna build mine out of bricks
         I'll work hard and I'll work long
         To make my house as strong as strong

She built that house in an hour and a day
And when she was done she thought

PIG 3   Say hey
         This brick house will
         keep that wolf away

She kicked up her hooves and did a roll
And into the front door she did stroll
Just then when the third little pig was done
The wolf came along feeling hungry

WOLF I am hungry and what I could dig
      Is a round little plump little
      Fat little pig

ALL PIGS Oink oink

Came the sounds as clear as a bell

WOLF Growl
      That's a pig I can tell
      What a sound what a smell

Gently he rapped
Softly he tapped
And with the widest possible grin

WOLF Open up piggy I know you're in

PIG 1 It's the wolf it's the wolf
       I can tell by the grin
       Not by the hairs on my chinny chin chin

WOLF Look little pig don't be a clown
Or I'll huff and I'll puff
And I'll blow your house down

PIG 1 I dare you I dare you

Taunted the first little pig
And the wolf . . . well . . . he did
That house that was built in a minute or two
Fell to the ground
Away it blew

WOLF Ah ha

Wheezed the wolf creasing with laughter
His heart all aglow in hungry rapture

WOLF *(running into Pig Number One's house)*
Hello little piggy
(no answer) Wait! Where can she be

PIG 1 *(hotfoots it over to Pig Number Two's house and knocks)*
Open up the door, brother, it's me

The wolf he was angry and went over and stood
In front of the second house made of wood
Just then two little pigs looked out

> WOLF   What joy what joy
>   Two pig snouts

The wolf he quivered with delicious delight

> WOLF   I can eat two piggies if I play things right
>   Open up darlings it's your mama pig

> PIGS 1 and 2   Can't fool us wolf Mama wears a wig

> WOLF   Open up the door pigs
>   Don't be clowns
>   Or I'll huff and I'll puff and
>   I'll blow your house down

> PIGS 1 and 2   Go on go on

>   Cried the two little pigs
>   And the wolf he did
>   That house that was built in a minute or three
>   Collapsed to the ground
>   For the world to see

WOLF AHHHHHHHHH

Wheezed the wolf his voice in song
But when he looked around the pigs were gone
(The two pigs run into the third house)
With a rage and a fury all over his face he cried

   WOLF They must be at the other place

He sneakily stalked over to see
When he eyed the pigs
One two three

   WOLF Raptures
         If I play things right
         I get to eat three pigs tonight
         Open up piggies it's your long lost brother

    PIG 3 We don't have another brother
          I already checked with mother

The wolf he stormed and ranted and swore
He pounded upon the brick house door

   WOLF Open up open up
         Let me in
ALL PIGS Not by the hairs on our
         chinny chin chins

WOLF   Then I'll huff and I'll puff and
             I'll blow your house in

ALL PIGS   We dare you We dare you

The wolf huffed and puffed but to no avail
He grunted and groaned until he was pale
He grew dizzy and staggered all around
Finally the wolf just collapsed on the ground

PIGS 1 and 2 Poor wolf

Whispered the pigs as they stepped outside
But just as they spoke
The wolf jumped up exclaiming JOKE

Around and around the three pigs fled
Around and around the four of them sped
The pigs escaped inside once more
And the wolf he howled
till his voice was sore

        PIG 3: Sister brother this plan I must call
               Here's how we get the wolf to fall
               I know we can do it
               We're a great team
PIGS 1 and 2 We are we are

They snorted with a gleam

PIG 3 Now use your brains
        Consult your wits
        We'll gather bits of straw and sticks
        And little sister up the chimney you must climb
        And poke out your head

PIG 1 I can do that just fine
        (She scampers up and pokes out her head)
        Oh Wooolllfff try to catch us this time

WOLF I'll get you I'll get you
        You're not hard to find

        Snarled the wolf as up on the roof he climbed
        The pigs lit the branches
        Till a fire burned hot
        On top of which they placed a huge pot

WOLF Dinner for me dinner for me
        Here I come piggies one two and three

The wolf leapt down the chimney
A mean gleam in his eye
Little did he know he was soon to die
For he met his sad end in a pot of hot water
He drowned and perished forever after
The three little pigs stood for a while

Then one by one each began to smile

From a smile to a grin

By their chinny chin chins

Till all you could see was a pile of pink wiggles

They kicked up their hooves

Rolled around on the floor

And lived together in that brick house

Forevermore

Sunflowers

Almost morning

beds of yellow petals

turning

stretching

at last

the sun rolls over

132

Bumblebees and hummingbirds

It was all
bumblebees and hummingbirds
crickets and swifts
till mulberry clouds
fat with March vapour
stung by wind
rumbled the sun
and a million raindrops
bounced petal to leaf to ground
as water sprang through rocks
braiding the earth in a torrent of
just-born rivers
a landslide of
mud-bubbling puddles
and in that downpour
that deluge
only one tiny cuckoo
hidden on a slippery wisp
of some barely
green branch
dared to sing

The Sun Queen

afternoon

She   Sun.

Sun   My Queen.

She   Where have you gone?

Sun   Behind the cloud.

She   Won't you come out?

Sun   I'm afraid I can't.

She   Is there nothing to do?

Sun   You could call the wind to move the cloud.

She   OK. Where is the wind?

Sun   Behind the rain.

She   Where is the rain?

Sun   Hidden in the cloud.

She   Which one?

Sun   I don't know. I can't see from here.

She   You play too many games.

Badger square dance

Now all join paws and circle round
Bow to your partner way 'cross town
Doh-see-doh and doh-see-dail
Swing your neighbour by the tail

Allemande left and allemande right
Promenade all through the night
Shoot the stars and stomp your feet
Flip your tails please make it neat

Whoopee doo and whoopee yikes
Every badger scratch his stripes
Outside couple change your gears
Nip your sweetheart on the ears

Single circle to an ocean wave
Wheel and deal and have a rave
Circulate around the world
Make sure your toes are nicely curled

Scoot on back and tag a line
Keep it up you're lookin' fine
Tea cup chain now don't cha fret
Slip the clutch right to your sett

Sashay low and sashay high
Sweep a quarter now don't be shy
Every badger in the crowd
Skip and hop and shout out loud

Whoopee tie yie tie yie oh
Catch your darlin' by the toe
Once you have him don't let go
Sing whoopee tie yie tie yie oh

The wild boar

When day is night,
night still day,
the dogs and I walk.

A narrow path threads the hill
behind our house.
Even in March it is baleful
obscured by tight fitting pines,
broody green oak.
It has rained for a month.
I avoid new pools
of dank wetness.
Mud oozes underfoot.

Sidestepping jagged rocks,
thorns stab my coat –
tiny feathers spring out.
Clusters of scratchy brush
cling to my pants.
I push aside spiky branches,
skeletal arms of last summer.
Like an unlit tunnel at the amusement park
unnamed things fly from strange places
and even just-sprung miniature jonquils
can't dispel the uneasy darkening haze.

I try to keep up with the dogs –
two shiny-eyed balls
caked in clotted dirt and
stringy dried vines
gargoyles of the forest.

Something's in the air
a loud scent summons.
The dogs take off,
race towards an emerald field of
spring wheat just rising.
They leap over gullies,
sail through tall grasses,
hawks circle – what's up?

I shout their names,
follow clumsily on two feet.
They ignore my calls and whistles.

Tangled in distant shadows
I spot it.

A great ragged beast
lured from sleep
who in one brazen shake
captures their spirits.

The dogs
forgetting all else
know nothing but the chase.

Only the chase.

But they can't keep up.
For this huge dark creature
with its outsized head
long snout
furred body moves
ever faster
ever lighter,
blurring into twilight.

Till breathing hard
it mounts the final crest
and pauses shadowless –
a heavy muscled silhouette,
triumphant
against an unyielding
primitive sky.

And the dogs
like me –
no match for such power.

Shivering crickets

As the ginger moon exits
in a final spring soak
shivering crickets
prepare to sing

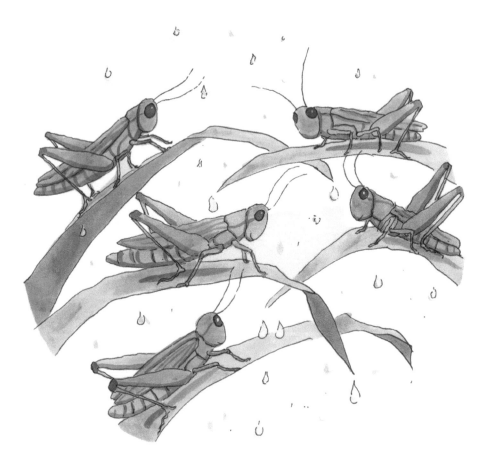

Badger's haiku

Burrow and dig
dig burrow
as the sun sinks low
earth rises

so sweet

When I was the grass

When I was
the grass
I bowed
to the wind

now that
I'm the mountain-top
no one can
tell me anything

When I was the wind

When I was the wind
I travelled
all the time

now that
I'm a rock
I have a lot
of time
inside of me

Our dog

Our dog barked all the time
each day he barked
forgetting how he barked
the day before
the first year he barked
with spring mud under his chin
and then in summer
when the mud had dried
he barked at the green snake
of the garden hose
he barked through the flying
of the autumn sycamore leaves
and barked circles
in the lighthearted snow

He barked at neighbourhood dogs cats
squirrels birds of any colour
at the children playing tag
at the snails soft bugs flies
lawnmower hums
anything

Then when spring came again
and the moist April earth
caked to the fringes of his fur
he died

Maybe it was too much for him
barking at the violets as they grew

The weed

a little play

Boy   Father. Come quick!

Father What is it, boy?
Is anything wrong?
What happened?

Boy   I did it!

Father Did what?

Boy   I pulled this weed out of the
ground.

Father That's good. You're very strong
today.

Boy   You bet I'm strong. I was pulling
one way, and the whole earth was
pulling the other way, and I won.

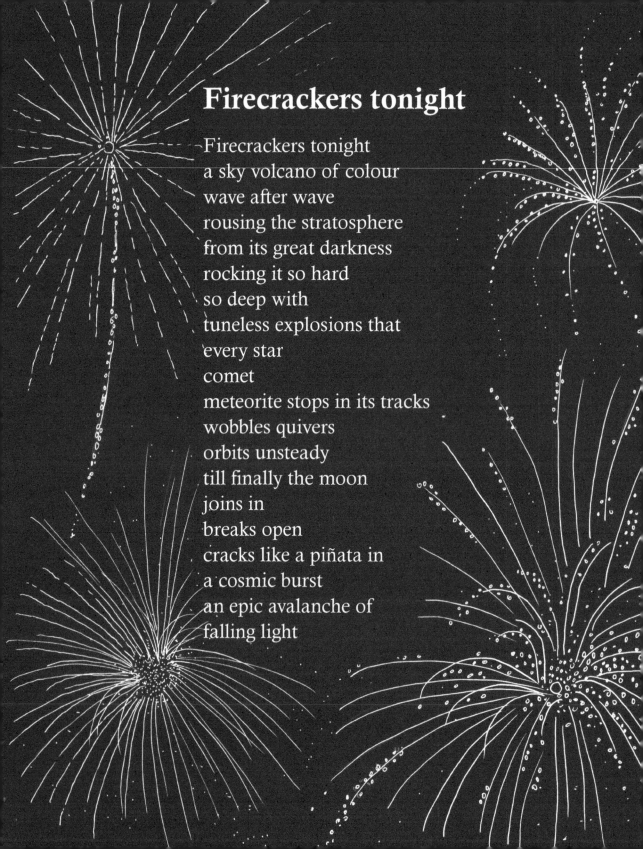

Firecrackers tonight

Firecrackers tonight
a sky volcano of colour
wave after wave
rousing the stratosphere
from its great darkness
rocking it so hard
so deep with
tuneless explosions that
every star
comet
meteorite stops in its tracks
wobbles quivers
orbits unsteady
till finally the moon
joins in
breaks open
cracks like a piñata in
a cosmic burst
an epic avalanche of
falling light

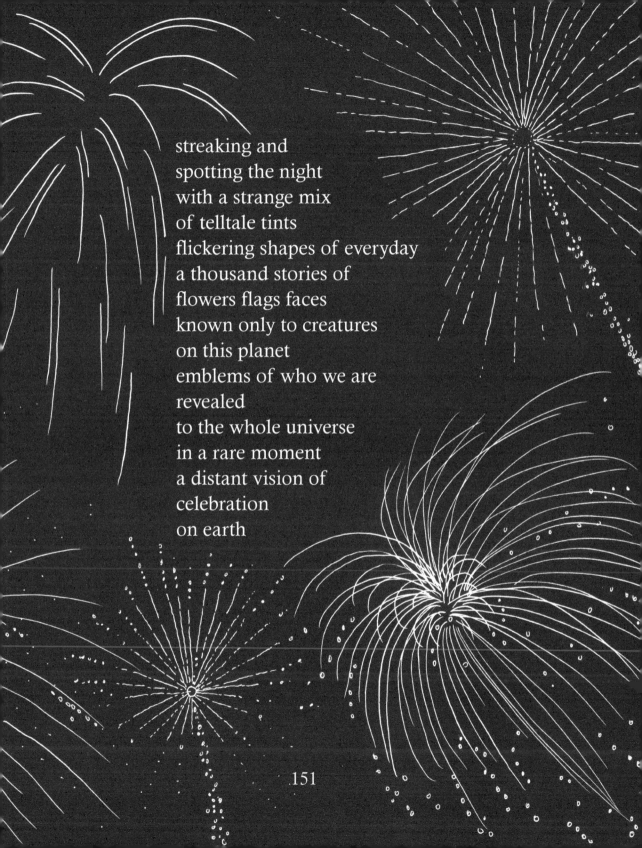

streaking and
spotting the night
with a strange mix
of telltale tints
flickering shapes of everyday
a thousand stories of
flowers flags faces
known only to creatures
on this planet
emblems of who we are
revealed
to the whole universe
in a rare moment
a distant vision of
celebration
on earth

I love you little snail
A tall tale Valentine ballad

I love you little snail, with your long slimy trail
though I know you think that I lie
when you sparkle on that rail
I waggle my tail
And these huge feet bounce up to the sky

(CHORUS)
Oh Saint Valentine
your name is ever sublime
there seldom are heard more encouraging words
than I love you come rain or come shine

Oh dear mumbled the snail whilst nibbling some kale
pachyderm you are quite a hunk
but cease all your hype
my dinner's getting ripe
and please do stop waving that trunk

For my heart lies with lark when she sings in the park
I'll never love any other
but I'm a spirally snail
without any tail
boo hoo I'm heading back home to mother

Ignoring the snail who fell into a pail
the lark gave a smile of pure rapture
who's that shaggy brown bear
oh what fabulous hair
chirp chirp his heart I must capture

The love of my dreams swims in this stream
growled the bear while chasing a fish
that pink salmon so fair
who never needs air
is my kind of beautiful dish

That salmon no doubt now wore a big pout
she didn't intend to be dinner
that bear was a thug
she shouted out UGH
I'm afraid you're about to get thinner

For I have a love he's called turtle dove
fills my slippery gills with gladness
now stop all your growling
and cease all that prowling
I leap with a love that's pure madness

But the dove as it goes was searching for toes
and the salmon just wouldn't do
there was simply no hope
that fish felt like a dope
so she swam back upstream, wouldn't you

If I had my druthers cooed the dove to the others
my heart would fly to that sloth
with three fabulous toes
my how slowly he goes
to sloth I must pledge my troth

Don't be silly sang sloth I'm in love with a moth
who flutters all over the place
we've met in the past
she's my sweetheart at last
and so fast she can win any race

Oh no cried the moth while destroying some cloth
I've engaged in deep contemplation
When I settle my tail
I'll land on that whale
our love just a cockeyed creation

The whale nodded in glee – going with me?
but oh little moth here's the worry
I am after all that
a fat acrobat
who's in love with somebody furry

Ahem purred the feline, it's true I'm divine
and that big whale is already smitten
But the truth is this cat
knows just where it is at
ouch, the love bug has bitten

When I spotted that goat, my poor heart was smote
I was trembling, all howls and cat calls
He looked wonderfully weird
with those hoofs and long beard
meow meow, does he notice me at all

Forget it cried goat, I'm an ordinary bloke
you cats are far too aloofy
with your noses in the air
like you don't even care
no creature is really so goofy

Romance is a joke, there I have spoke
this love stuff ridiculous and silly
I'd rather have me a blast
chomping on grass
don't ever forget I'm called Billy

Everything stopped, the bubble had popped
was love truly a stupid fat bore
they all were bemused
frustrated confused
licking their wounds feeling sore

It was over and done, love was no longer fun
romance had gone out on their part
Till one cold winter's day
St Valentine passed their way
dressed in white lace and a big candy heart

Now this saint was smart, had a most special art
with his bow aimed love arrows to fly
as the chocolate love darts
zinged straight to each heart
everyone voiced a huge sigh

Next a chorus unfurled, every sound in the world
till all creatures grinned with delight
marry me one did blurt
your ears are so pert
romance had flown back that night

Each laughed as they crooned a most wonderful tune
as true love did light up the sky
from the snails to the larks
they sang with full hearts
and nobody stopped to ask why

That saint he did wink and blush pretty pink
and murmured one last little fact
tonight please don't miss
landing that kiss
remember opposites do attract

(CHORUS)
Oh Saint Valentine
your name is ever sublime
there seldom are heard more encouraging words
than I love you come rain or come shine

Horse

What is it you hear horse
when you arch your head
to the ground
is there a story
of brown
of green
in the sweet clotted earth you inhale
in the feather grass that brushes your cheek

What is it you see horse
when you run along that crack
of land
of sky
tell me
for I too long to part the wind
with my head
for I too ache for a story

Questions and answers

Q What's inside the sun?
A Daytime

Q What's inside the earth?
A Colours before they get their names.

Q Who made the first circle?
A Someone who got very dizzy.

Q What draws the bee to the honeysuckle?
A Ten million summers.

Q What roars inside a seashell?
A Beach lions.

Q What roars inside you?
A My blood.

Q How does one tie a rainbow?
A The first thing is to find the ends.

Q If it's noon here, what time is it on Mars?
A A billion years before noon.

Q How long does it take to move a mountain?
A Depends on the number of ants available.

Q At what speed does a moth move to a lamp?
A At light speed.

Q Why is the letter I dotted?
A To have a good time?

Waiting

Sometimes
I wait too long
for the next thing
to happen
and when that
happens I'm
waiting for the
next thing to happen

now I
could either

A: Keep waiting for the next thing to happen
or
B: Keep happening and not wait at all

Winter

Winter
hold your breath
this air is
mud fresh
and runs thick with spring
and deep with the scent
of lilac

Winter
if you only
knew what lay ahead
you'd never have
opened your mouth
at all this year

The back of beyond

Twilight holds dominion here
and for a certain time
in certain months
night is never really dark
daytime never really gone
and the full moon just an afterthought

Strange forces gather at such moments
rituals of shadow play
feats of illusion

Blurry silhouettes
seagulls on crinkled swells
bob and roll towards my tiny window

Dark water laps hungrily against the shore
crease by crease coastline vanishes
as if the rocky headland by the cottage
carpeted by rusty sea tangle
was never there

And even the speckled brown seals
with little dog faces
who had been sun-preening
on their lichen stone beds
and feasting on rock fish
have vanished

They say that some can see farther
in the back of beyond
that they
like the moon
can turn the tide when they wish
talk to wild cats
or befriend a swan

But perhaps only at twilight
when the sky like the water has no edge
hours have no markings
and when the flame from the candle
I burn on the dining table
eventually goes out

Three deer

Following
some early morning ritual
three deer softly leap across
the narrow lane
just in front of me

I am pedalling like a racing hare
when my bike mysteriously slows

It stops

Squinting through the glare
I am not sure
but I think the deer
look back

Dinosaur site

So many hairpin turns,
such a winding road —
it must have drifted to earth
from another era,
landing fold after fold
like a silk ribbon
between the pines.

I climb higher.
Distant shapes before me
ripen into summer mountains.
A few crescent-thin wings
trace the day's first filigrees
over an imperfect chorus of summits
smudged fresh morning green.

The rocks, slopes, trees
all striped —
now sun, now shadow
shadow sun —
like some ancient flag of a forgotten age
where distance is meaningless,
time unheard of.

Then all at once I pass a sign,
'Dinosaur Site'.
Dinosaurs?
Dinosaurs?

And following that same ribbon,
that same trail,
I arrive here
two hundred million years ago.

Great beasts stalk everywhere —
armour-coated and spiked,
their snaking long necks
on the lookout always.
Like players in some prehistoric film
they sway and swagger cartoon-like,
roaming through twisted forests
of tall pines,
ginkgo trees,
spiny growing things.

Newborn wind is swept aside
by their enormous tails as
they make their way, open-jawed,

over flat land —
digging in those colossal scaly feet
and etching with each step
mile low valleys,
mile high peaks.
Banding together they search,
food, shelter, mates
fighting to the death till
parched throats ache.

Angry now,
they dig for water.
The ground flies up
disturbed and wounded.
It spins without pause into dark hills
as rivers gush from some
bottomless place
till poor earth
can take it no more.
The land rumbles and cracks,
breaks apart into vast smoking clods —
continents.

For these giants
are in charge of the world —
where I am a dot of the future
invisible and without a scent.

Unimportant in a scene
heaving with tuneless cries,
furious with mud and dust,
an unyielding theatre of the past
and like a myth
marking the planet

indelibly.

The hare, the pheasant and the sparrow

The hare jumps
across the
white frost field
so sure
a summer river

A rust and polished
pheasant
swoops low
through mist
with shrills
to clear his path

Sparrow
sits on the stone wall
does he know
thousands have come
before him

A trade

I'll trade you my kingdom for your song

I'll trade you my song for your colour

I'll trade you my colour for your story

I'll trade you my story for your dance

I'll trade you my dance for your daydream

I'll trade you my daydream for your hand

I'll trade you my hand for your hand

Cherry blossoms

Cherry blossoms

are quiet

unlike frogs

leaping to every

raindrop

If it were my birthday

If it were my birthday
I'd be the bounce of a basketball
or the stretch of a telephone call
I'd wrap up in a waterfall

I'd jump in and out
of somersaults
and fall into a spin
and spin another grin

If it were my birthday
I'd be the shine of a hummingbird's flight
or the shimmy of a wild horse fight
I'd be the silk of a bonfire light

this makes me laugh
dandelion puffs
this makes me think
in zigzags

179

When I was the sky

When I was
the
sky
I
collected
airplanes
balloons
rockets
mosquitoes
birds
kites
planets
meteors
clouds
flies
and dust

now that
I'm
the
earth
I
wonder
how
I
got
so
much
air

When I was the forest

When I was
the
forest
it took me
one hundred years
to have a thought

now that
I'm the sea
I can change
my mind
in a second

My eyes

My eyes
rush to the stream

while
my feet take me to
the rest of the day

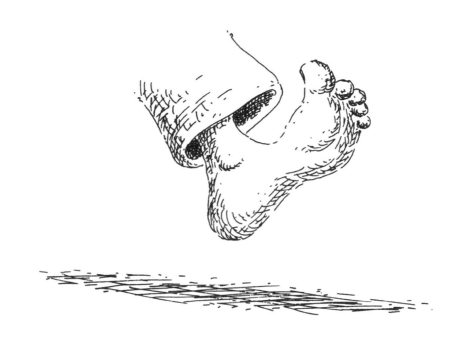

Unicorn

Unicorn
don't go
let me ask you
how long you've been here

please
no lies

An October wind

An October wind
ruffles the heavy shade of
the summer maple

Its leaves grow
lightheaded and
drop off in a million
crimson circles

The tree is an
outline of itself
good for
unruffling the wind

The ladybird

Remember me?
I'm the
ladybird that
tiptoed
down
your
thumb
the afternoon
that you
turned one

What?
No?

I
guess you
were asleep

Shadows

Moon
last evening you
rolled so loud and silver
past my window
that the shadows
woke and wove their dark
molasses stripes
over my bed
and
in the criss-cross of
that night-time
I knew what to do
breathe soft
breathe soft
and fold into a
quiet silhouette
until morning

My dog

When
my dog
sleeps by the fire

not even a
tangerine fox
can rouse her

The first crocus

Oh
the first crocus
others must be hidden
in the snowy folds
of March

Mud

It squelches and belches
a spattering flop
a morass of dense goop
that gurges in glops

Now seeping now weeping
a popple a spurt
a lagoon of brown pudding
some very wet dirt

It burbles so blustery
and spills out its custardy
bubbles that pop
from bottom to top

To squeeze between toes
and squish as it goes
all oozy and flabby
dank deep and slabby

Oh
no
so
slow

What a lazy muddle
what a hiccup of a puddle

When I was a mouse

When I was
a
mouse
darkness
circled
above
my
head
like
a
hawk

When I was a dragon

When I was

a

dragon

I

spit

burning

fire words

and

in

the

smoke

I

could

see

no

one

Ten minute poem

There are only ten minutes left to go
should I get up and get ready to leave now
or should I keep doing this for nine minutes more
or climb a tree in eight minutes
or bake a cake in seven minutes
or write a book in six minutes
or make an important scientific discovery
during the next five minutes
or compose a symphony in four minutes
or save my country in three minutes
or circumnavigate the globe in two minutes
or explore the milky way in one minute
or or or or or . . . .

Me and the earthworm

a very very short play

Me	Where are you going, earthworm?
Earthworm	Around the world
Me	How long will that take
Earthworm	A long stretch

The Sun Queen

evening

She	And Sun
Sun	My Queen
She	You may not leave
Sun	Why is that?
She	Night-time grows shadows
Sun	But night-time grows stars
She	All right. Goodnight Sun.
	And Moon?
Moon	Yes?
She	No tricks tonight.
Moon	Good night your majesty.

Fireflies

If
you collect
enough fireflies
you could
read secrets
under your blanket
all night long

It's easy to dream

It's easy to dream
just wait for
evening
to powder the sky
with a million thoughts

and then
select a few for yourself

Night sky

Night sky
floods my room
oh
my heart pounds
the moon is
now my own